图书在版编目（CIP）数据

海棠怒放：汉、英 / 霍红著 . -- 青岛：中国海洋
大学出版社，2025. 2. -- ISBN 978-7-5670-4067-0

Ⅰ. I227

中国国家版本馆 CIP 数据核字第 2025A891M4 号

出版发行	中国海洋大学出版社			
社　　址	青岛市香港东路 23 号		**邮政编码**	266071
出 版 人	刘文菁			
网　　址	http://pub.ouc.edu.cn			
订购电话	0532 - 82032573（传真）			
责任编辑	邵成军		**电　　话**	0532 - 85902533
印　　制	青岛海蓝印刷有限责任公司			
版　　次	2025 年 2 月第 1 版			
印　　次	2025 年 2 月第 1 次印刷			
成品尺寸	170 mm ×230 mm			
印　　张	11. 75			
字　　数	42 千			
印　　数	1—1 000			
定　　价	89. 00 元			

霍红

作者简介

　　2001 年成都理工大学英语专业毕业,获文学学士学位;2005 年澳大利亚莫纳什大学国际英语教学专业毕业,获教育学硕士学位;2013 年 12 月至 2014 年 12 月在美国俄克拉何马州立大学英语系访学;2015 年上海外国语大学英语语言文学专业毕业,获博士学位;2015 至 2021 年,于扬州大学文学院做博士后。现为扬州大学外国语学院副教授、硕士生导师。主要学术兴趣包括文学翻译、语用学及二语习得。系江苏省翻译工作者协会会员。主持江苏省教育厅哲学社会科学研究项目 1 项,出版教材 2 部,出版《海棠依旧·霍红双语诗集选》自创自译中英双语格律诗著作 1 部,出版《英韵经典唐诗百首》译著 1 部,多篇翻译作品在《英语世界》等期刊发表。

The Author's Profile

Huo Hong, who received a Bachelor's degree in English literature from Chengdu University of Technology in 2001, a Master's degree in TESOL from Monash University, Australia in 2005, a doctoral degree in English language and literature from Shanghai International Studies University in 2015 and who was a visiting scholar to the English department of Oklahoma State University, the US from the December 2013 to that of 2014 and was doing postdoctoral research at College of Humanities of Yangzhou University from 2015 to 2021, is now an associate professor of College of International Studies of Yangzhou University, who supervises postgraduates and whose academic interest covers literary translation, pragmatics and second language acquisition. As a member of Jiangsu Translators Association, she is found productive in books and research papers, has undertaken one provincial project funded by Educational Department of Jiangsu Province and was involved in compiling two textbooks. Keen on translating traditional Chinese poems though, she has translated some literary works such as English-translated essays published in *The English World*. More than what relates to her career, she is a poet who has had a poem selection of her own published, namely *Gone and Go On* in both Chinese and English, with her translated work *Classic Tang Poems in English Rhyme* lately published.

序

  诗人的人生是人生，诗人的人生也是诗。忙忙碌碌中，平平淡淡中，我们体察秋愁冬郁，品出人情冷暖，将生活中的平凡诉诸文字，抒发对人生无常的感叹，或激扬，或惆怅，或几度欢愉，或几段高调嚣张。不惑之年解人生之秘，天命之年可是必听天由命？随遇而安、顺其自然是一解，然，总会有些许不甘。

  任这世界喧嚣浮躁，任我的心一如既往地高傲。曾经霜打的斑驳，被我心的高傲修补，曾经重击而铸的含蓄，被我心的高傲消除。它在我的生命中流淌，让我不再彷徨，令我不甘安然。美丽的，构筑我生命中的阳光，照耀我，温暖我；冷酷的，迫我前行，笞我逃之夭夭，亦是于我有益。人心虽易伤，人心也易愈，愈则百炼成钢。

  当人生即将过半，当往事常忆心头，曾经的春花即残、烈夏炎苦、秋帐吁叹以及冬夜难眠，正如往日云烟随风逐渐消散。当人生不惑，看淡是认命，释然是服输，然而与每一个字灵共舞的心不变。当"骤雨已歇"而"海棠依旧"，便不再以字载忧、以文录愁，从此文字是铿锵的、坚定的、掷地有声的，为不屈从天命，为骨血中的倔强，我的人生方向就在每一首诗里。

  无韵不诗，诗乐相通。韵是美的途径，缠绵温柔或大气磅礴，是韵，也是格律。格律诗词在字数、韵脚、平仄、对仗各方面都有讲究，文字凝练，是中国古代文体的最高体式。本书收录了作者的169首格律诗词以及几首散曲，并配以格律体的译文，其中有一部分诗词来自作者的上一部双语诗集《海棠依旧》，并配以对这部分诗词重译的译诗，借以表达对祖国传统诗歌的热爱及敬意，"以诗译诗"，也期待未来有机会在世界范围内传播该诗歌译体。

本书收录的 169 首诗（或词或散曲），多以自然景物为题，兼有爱国、怀人等主题，是作者心境与思想的容器，有甜有咸，有情有志，包含五言绝句、七言绝句、七言律诗以及多种词牌的词，及其英文译文。译诗讲求格律和韵，仿十四行诗体，韵格为"aabb（cc…）""abab（ab…）""aaba"以及"aaaa（aa…）"等形式。

本书系全国首部自创自译的（近体）诗词集《海棠依旧》的续篇，作者即译者，所有诗词均由作者创作，所有的译文均由作者翻译。中华文化博大精深，中国的汉字有灵有魂，携其之手，与字灵共舞，让我的生命在文字中存在，幸甚至哉！以另一种语言，以诗译诗，令中华的文化借以传播。祖国的文字，如晖如曦，应有月与其辉映，让月传递日的光辉。

本书获得中国海洋大学出版社责任编辑邵成军主任的大力支持以及扬州大学出版基金资助，特此感谢。

霍 红

2024 年 9 月 16 日于扬州

 Preface

The poet lives a life; the poet lives a poem. Through hustle and bustle of life, the poet tends to perceive the gloom in weathered hardships, feel social warmth and coldness, and resort to Chinese characters or words to heave a sigh for the uncertain ones out of the common occurrences, which may unfold themselves in an inspiring or depressed or sometimes enjoyable or oftentimes unconstrained fashion. In one's forties, one solves the mystery of life; as one is to go on his fifty, will he or she have to succumb to his or her fate? Reconciliation with the supernatural life design is a resolution to refer to, which, however, he derives somehow from suppressed volition.

Let the earth alone in hustle and restlessness, and let me bear a lofty heart, which restores the wounded to health and substitutes timidity with confidence and the loftiness of which flows in the river of my life, dragging me away from oscillation and arming me with a burst of great expectations. Whatever is lofty in nature builds up the sunshine in my life, which floods over me, warming me up; whatever is gloomy urges me forward, lashing me with the whip of gloom to the rise of a thought of being released, which is to the good of mine in the matter of fact. Not only is a heart prone to hurt, but to heal as well, which leads to its transformation into toughened and hardened steel then.

As one comes in the middle of his life where the past events or trivials are more often called to mind, all the ever ephemeral flowers, the savage summer heat, the autumn-borne woes and the insomnia-prone winter are vanishing into the wind. In one's forties, to take things lightly is a resignation to fate and to feel released of troubles is submission to the predetermined life. Whatever it is, the heart to dance with the character-carried elves remains. When the life storm was over and "the begonia" has the chance to have a sustained life, she is not likely any more to transport gloom and woe via Chinese characters or words to the readers, which, in reverse, show themselves up in the affirmative, firm and aggressive manner. In a bid not to give herself up to the life predetermined by some supernatural power and to cleave to her obstinacy in the blood, she designs her life in and between her lines.

Rhymeless is no poetry, which is closely tied up with music. Rhyme is the approach to musical charm, whose gentle grace, grandeur and pomp stem from the rhyme as well as the metre. Metrical poems and lyrics, which enjoy elegance and terseness and need to meet the requirements of the limited number of a line or an entire poem/lyric, rhyming, use of tone and antithesis, are considered as the best recognized ancient Chinese literary style. Aimed at expressing my ardent love, paying respects to the ancient Chinese poetry and spreading the pattern of translating poems into English in metre and rhyme, this book includes a selection of 169 pieces, metrical poems, lyrics and several songs (verses popular in the Yuan Dynasty with the use of metres and rhyme), which are translated into English in metre and rhyme and some of which come from my former poem collection *Gone and Go On* and are retranslated into English in the same fashion.

The recorded 169 pieces of poetry (or in the form of lyrics or short Yuan songs), largely themed on natural scenes as well as some concerned with patriotism and a recollection of friends, are containers that hold the poet's emotions and thoughts, either sweet or bitter, either moody or ambitious, including metrical quatrains and octaves and lyrics to a range of tunes in both Chinese and English. The translation is done in metre and rhyme primarily after the fashion of the sonnet, with the rhyme in the patterns of "aabb(cc...)" "abab(ab...)". It is also done in other patterns the way the ancient Chinese poems rhyme, such as "aaba" and "aaaa(aa...)".

This book is a sequel to *Gone and Go On*, the first book of metrical poems and lyrics authored and translated by the same person in China, the author of which is the translator herself—poems and lyrics are written and translated into English by Dr. Huo Hong herself. The Chinese culture covers an extended range of elements, among which are the Chinese characters that have their respective souls, dancing with which allows my sustenance through the Chinese characters. A great blessing it is! In another tongue, the Chinese culture enjoys a big chance of spreading by means of poems in English with metre and rhyme. As can be understood, the glow of Chinese characters has every right to be reflected through the sheen of the English words.

I hereby extend my warmest gratitude to Mr. Shao Chengjun with China Ocean University Press for his painstaking effort committed to the publication of the book and to Publication Fund of Yangzhou University.

Huo Hong
September 16, 2024 in Yangzhou

目 录

海棠怒放

如梦令（其一）

一树绿垂茎瘦，

日晒叶间斑锈。

择尽主枝留，

却又幸福依旧。

知否？知否？

眉蹙翠穷时候。

Like a Dream (No. 1)

Out of life became the green plant;

With sunburned leaves, the twigs did slant.

Leaves taken off around,

Again, she got alive and sound.

Do you know? Do you know?

I frowned oft when she lost her glow.

如梦令（其二）

余目绿荫织就，
恣眺远方仙岫。
闲憩对轩窗，
此景年年都有。
依旧。依旧。
我处绿肥红瘦。

Like a Dream (No. 2)

With a glimpse at the shade of green,
Looking up at the hilly scene,
I sit by the window right here,
Which comes at this time of each year.
It stays so. It stays so.
In my eyes are green and red glow.

如梦令（其三）

常见沿山河处，
三两水间白鹭。
偶遇在河边，
转眼驾云腾雾。
难渡。难渡。
是否蓬莱仙路。

Like a Dream (No. 3)

The Yanshan River often held in view,
On the water are egrets one or two.
Met with at the bank, they swim by,
They rose to cloud in the blink of an eye.
Hard to go, hard to go.
Is it the path to Heaven, do you know?

如梦令（其四）

总见雨疏风骤，
应是洞天别有。
试抚绪先生，
人竟比黄花瘦。
知否？知否？
辛苦至今依旧。

Like a Dream (No. 4)

With rains and winds seen frequently,
A wonderful spot there should be.
To calm my heart I try;
To be thinner than all am I.
Do you know? Do you know?
Till now on life pains I still go.

如梦令（其五）

雨润远山他处，
雷打岸前门户。
楼外有听闻，
杜宇声声不住。
难赋，难赋。
孟母蓬莱仙术。

Like a Dream (No. 5)

In far hills and beyond rain pours;
To windows and doors thunder roars.
Out the windows what's heard:
The bird's cuckoos and cuckoos stirred.
Hard to write, hard to write,
Is a mother's upbringing plight.

如梦令（其六）

蓝幕茫茫艳昼，
一路东行寻旧。
细数已十年，
少女伊时还幼。
太久，太久。
又见桂花凡柳。

Like a Dream (No. 6)

On a bright day, skies vast and blue,
We walk east the old way all through.
Since last, ten years it's been:
Two years old the young girl was seen,
Long ago, long ago.
To th' eye osmanthus 'nd willows go.

如梦令（其七）

湿地绿萍白鹭，
穷碧纤荷一幕。
夏至往来寻，
雏鸟何时高骛？
飞入，飞入。
当是白云深处！

Like a Dream (No. 7)

Marsh, weeds, and the egrets have been
Part of the lily pad pond scene.
Egret chicks I come for;
When did they soar off, here no more?
In solo flight, in double flight,
The birds rise behind the clouds white.

如梦令（其八）

河映云疏帷幕，
腾雾南来秋处，
但问眼前人，
总道沧桑歧路。
留步，留步。
还我蔚蓝一宿。

Like a Dream (No. 8)

The cloud reflections in the rill are few.
Fog from the north adds to the autumn view.
Let me just ask those before you,
Who'll not say change in life is always true?
Stop the hue, stop the hue;
Return us for one day the sky so blue.

采桑子（其一）

东风携雨秋分过，
日月如梭。
日月如梭，
又见黄花香桂多。

凉蟾桂子中秋色，
夜里衾薄。
夜里衾薄，
又对新寒待与说。

Gathering Mulberries (No. 1)

East wind with rain, fall equinox has passed;
Time and tide have flown past.
Time and tide have flown past.
Seen again is the patch of gold blooms vast.

Bright and cold is the Mid-autumn Moon ray;
In the night chill I stay.
In the night chill I stay.
Cold of another year, with whom to say?

采桑子（其二）

和风曛日葳蕤醉，
愿语千重。
赏碧葱葱，
一度常常喜艳彤。

明轩方几离离对，
感浸香浓。
沐翠朦胧，
此去独独爱淡红。

Gathering Mulberries (No. 2)

Drunk by the warm breeze, dusk sun, and the green,
All with poetic sheen,
Watching the verdant flow,
I think of my ever love for red glow.

The plant laid somewhere even to a height,
Steeped in the plant delight,
With green plants in the room,
I would just have a life in lesser gloom.

采桑子(其三)

雨初如注雷随后,
水洗微尘。
荡醉千痕,
霖塑涛波休旧陈。

常吟山雨楼中色,
朱雀罗门。
夏仲如焚,
不愿当歇处处涔。

Gathering Mulberries (No. 3)

Followed by thunders, first comes rain,

Washing away the dust,

Taking away my pain,

For a life change one has a lust.

Oft I chant hill lanes in the rain,

The vermilion gates' rust,

And a summer so plain.

There's no after-rain mess, I trust.

采桑子(其四)

霞红风暖临行夜，
明月一弯。
把酒千言，
坐叙西亭此最欢。

乡愁一点独独作，
众友归三。
意兴阑珊，
我又西楼孤落单。

Gathering Mulberries (No. 4)

In the breezy gold evening glow,
The moon's in the sky bright.
Sharing wine 'nd what we know,
We sit around with our hearts light.

On nostalgia I write, alone;
Three friends have gone back home.
Very homesickness-prone,
Again I'm on my own in Rome.

采桑子（其五）

凡尘溢苦沉秋夜，
来去丹红。
又近寒冬，
黄叶萧萧与去重。

其实久已生华发，
时过匆匆。
惚恍眠中，
总见那年春日容。

Gathering Mulberries (No. 5)

A bitter life is lived on the fall night;
Flowers blossom aright.
Winter again on th' way,
Brown leaves rustle away the shiny day.

Indeed, the hair has been gray for so long;
Time has flashed all along.
In the bemusing dream,
Frequently seen is th' young face in a beam.

采桑子（其六）

金镶火染城西处，
一路彤彤。
片片当空，
暮色微调卷卷中。

群芳过后扬州好，
秋入残红。
心绪蒙蒙，
时过一般曲正浓。

Gathering Mulberries (No. 6)

The city is hued with fire in the west;
Red all way is the best.
Heaps of clouds in the air,
At dusk they are mincing along with care.

As blooms fall, good days linger in my place;
Autumn comes but in grace.
Are you still in the dark?
Middle-aged though, we are halfway with spark.

采桑子（其七）

凭栏独赏天为幕，
不见纤尘。
朵朵浮云，
寥廓苍穹初作吟。

丹心空也无颜色，
岁月留痕。
梦里缘寻，
莫负当闲一度今。

Gathering Mulberries (No. 7)

Alone against the rail I watch the sky,
No fine dust to the eye,
Clouds upon clouds on th' wing,
The vast firmament first for me to sing.

I have not a mind to win any race;
Time and tide leave a trace.
I follow in my dream;
Let me not idle such a gleam.

采桑子（其八）

寒风吹日千千尺，
深雾高阳。
浓霭成裳，
无处行寻庭外芳。

秋诗一两穷思尽，
无语成行。
残景茫茫，
待作新词慨而慷。

Gathering Mulberries (No. 8)

Blown thousands of inches up in the sky,
Fog heavy, the sun high,
Thick fog cloaks everywhere;
Then flowers aren't to be sought anywhere.

One or two fall poems could exhaust my mind;
No more words I can find.
With the bleak winter scene,
I am likely to have a rhyme so clean.

采桑子（其九）

百川九水逶迤去，
浩瀚纹波。
玉岫沿河，
叠嶂青峦处处多。

苍苍袤宇云霄下，
华夏当歌。
探月嫦娥，
寻梦千年说祖国。

Gathering Mulberries (No. 9)

The rills and rivers are winding their way,

Waves and vast billows gray.

Along run mountains green;

Hills and peaks all the way many are seen.

Between the azure heaven and vast earth,

China has proved her worth.

To the moon Chang'e flew;

The thousand-year-long dream man's sought comes true.

春日小记（其一）

昼长夜短九春忙，
窗外白华玉坠长。
一场如冬携冷雨，
朦胧化作两三行。

A Diary on a Spring Day (No. 1)

With day long and night short, spring's rushed along.
May the magnolia out the house last long.
A shower of wintry rain brings back cold.
My loss of mind is in lines to unfold.

春日小记（其二）

梅还未落玉兰开，
寒去刚刚春乍来。
一场霏霏夹雪雨，
两行成墨尽开怀。

A Diary on a Spring Day (No. 2)

Plum blossoms in bloom, magnolia has thrived.
Cold has not gone far and spring has arrived.
A shower of rain mixed with flying snow
Puts me to pen for my pleasure to grow.

鹧鸪天（其一）

新翠碧微鸣鸟栖，

日高风卷嫩枝低。

还寒乍暖初三月，

身裹冬衣独不急。

草染玉，杳离离，

河边垂列柳依依。

何须深浅不同色，

织彩葳蕤去岸西。

A Partridge in the Sky (No. 1)

Renewed green on trees, where birds sit atop,

The sun high, the branch droops until winds stop.

As March begins, cold and warmth in the air,

Uneager to dress light, I dress warm 'nd fair.

Grass jade green, far and wide,

Lined with willows, to th' distance the banks glide.

Why do you seek differently-shaded green?

By the river unfolds the best spring scene.

鹧鸪天（其二）

浅浅斜光暖碧萍，
新芽柳翠舞丹青。
堂前忙筑盘双燕，
檐下衔泥啾几声。

南往北，鸟长情，
归来还入旧屋庭。
盈盈偶落兰枝上，
袅袅一行微羽轻。

A Partridge in the Sky (No. 2)

The sunlight slants warm over the nature,
Over willow sprouts—a painted picture!
Above th' lounge, a swallow couple mend nest;
Under th' eaves, they carry clay 'nd chirp no rest.

Back from South, of love grace,
When back, they return to th' old dwelling place.
Found perching lithe in the magnolia tree,
They spiral up into the air with glee.

鹧鸪天（其三）

初上华灯只影孤，
千行万字一人读。
独身潜作六七卷，
相伴填词三两出。

书旧句，赋新株，
来回几首淡虚无。
忽闻嗔恨嘤嘤叹，
悲喜红尘件件疏。

A Partridge in the Sky (No. 3)

Lights just put on, she's at the desk alone,
Reading and writing all words on her own.
Buried in papers, many she does do;
In company, I write a poem or two.

In old lines, on spring trees,
I make light of all in poems two or three.
Suddenly an upset sigh comes about,
When her mind hustles earthly matters out.

鹧鸪天（其四）

款款沿山河岸行，
无边幕幕色初青。
眼前袅袅花出景，
足下葱葱草入屏。

三叶草，碧瑶瑛，
春风向北曳相迎。
夕阳晖里寻吉运，
默默告求四叶灵。

A Partridge in the Sky (No. 4)

As we pace down the Yanshan River slow,
The unending green's just started to grow.
Into the eye is the blossoming scene,
Beneath the feet comes the grass-woven screen.

Three-leafed clovers, green green to sway,
In north spring wind they nod to touch the clay.
For a four-leafed clover in th' setting sun,
I pray silently that she can find one.

鹧鸪天（其五）

皓皓萧萧月渐高，
穿肠酒肉亦风骚。
两盘家凤逢心意，
一口冰红弄酒豪。

霞晕染，面如烧，
喃喃低语敞心聊。
犹如只曲清平调，
旖旎低吟醉彻宵。

A Partridge in the Sky (No. 5)

Bright, the moon is climbing high in the sky,
With wine and meat, a poem I live and try.
Two plates of dainties meet my earthly need,
And a sip of wine to myself I feed.

Rosy cheeks, red in th' face,
Heart-to-heart words we had in rhythmic grace.
As if I were just listening to a tune,
I have in my lifetime one night to croon.

鹧鸪天（其六）

三月芳菲醉玉庭，
疏风袭木落丹瑛。
船边又见鸬鹚坐，
河上初怜白鹭惊。

千动影，万流轻，
涓涓细淌赋春声。
年年惆怅词中看，
一缕禅心不了情。

A Partridge in the Sky (No. 6)

With march fragrance the garden gives a glow;
Petals fall when a sudden wind does blow.
By banks cormorants again wait to fish;
While scared, up egrets on the river swish.

Dancing shadows, frolicking waves,
The river trickles down: for spring one craves.
Years upon years of sorrows in the line
Never end any breath of love of mine.

鹧鸪天（其七）

储秀万千俏海棠，
夺魂耀目画春妆。
朵中红粉盛黄蕊，
花外苞青筑乐房。

花簇簇，枝轻扬，
风华最久入文章。
潇潇玉雨绯绯落，
化作丹泥土更香。

A Partridge in the Sky (No. 7)

With thousands of blooms, th' begonia is fair;
Dazzling, she is in her stunning spring wear.
Tender yellow pistils contained inside,
The green leaves surround them at the outside.

In clusters, the twigs light,
Blossoms last longest in poems: a fine sight.
But a rustling rain beats them down aground;
Red clay smelling fragrant gets all around.

鹧鸪天（其八）

几丝残寒刺骨凉，
斜阳高照宛中央。
涌集红粉千波起，
吹散翠丹万缕香。

阴飒飒，冷轻扬，
萧萧数月沐沧桑。
徐徐阵阵东西去，
旖旎和风笔墨长。

A Partridge in the Sky (No. 8)

A chill in the air makes one freezing cold,
While the warm sun rays through the sky unfold.
Waves upon waves of red and pink come up,
As breaths upon breaths of fragrance spread up.

Winds soughing, cold all out,
Months of changes they do murmur about.
To the east or the west gusts of winds blow;
Gentle breezes come to a rhythmic show.

鹧鸪天（其九）

漫漫花笺园里拆，

无闻默默教人猜。

初惊一片花千计，

再探多重株百开。

三月赏，上旬栽，

春风料峭洗尘埃。

斜光日下六七照，

二月兰名记起来。

A Partridge in the Sky (No. 9)

An expanse of violets unfolds vast;

We can't tell what the name is, walking past.

We wonder at th' great expanse at first sight;

At such a small number at further sight.

Displayed in March, grown in June fair,

With a chilly wind, it cleans th' campus air.

After a few photos taken at all,

February Violet, we do recall.

鹧鸪天（其十）

昨日雨濯今艳红，
以为新种沐春风。
吹摇身曳娇娇异，
拂跃枝飞袅袅同。

一朵朵，两丛丛，
娟娟隔岸画朦胧。
海棠嫣媚不暇目，
怎教琳琅满眼空。

A Partridge in the Sky (No. 10)

Washed by yesterday's rain, they are so bright,
Looking freshly grown, bathed in a breeze light.
Blown to sway and strain, fine in different ways,
Fondled to bounce and bend, lithe in like rays.

Blooms upon blooms, clustered in two,
Gauze across the river can be seen through.
Begonia allows no rest of one's eyes
That must have access to where beauty lies.

鹧鸪天（其十一）

束束暖阳照海棠，
粉红独醉未闻香。
万株丹朵落闲地，
千寸绯泥纺绮裳。

霞晕染，任飞芳，
天生绝色恨难藏。
红尘滚滚长流去，
研墨君读又几行。

A Partridge in the Sky (No. 11)

On begonia shoot columns of sun-light;
Fragrance beyond smell, just pink comes in sight.
Petals swirl down on th' earth cheery and gay.
They render the land attired in red clay.

Like red clouds, a sweet tide,
She has stunning beauty that must not hide.
As time and tide go by like th' river flow,
I write on her in poetry, you'll know.

鹧鸪天(其十二)

风乍戚戚几日明，
绯绯嵌碧漫华庭。
一瞥花曳娟娟色，
再看枝摇袅袅形。

葱翠叶，舞娉婷，
繁华不慕绿长青。
海棠连夜经微雨，
玉立盈盈对北风。

A Partridge in the Sky (No. 12)

Winds in whispers, sunny days few,
Pink set in green comes into view,
First rushes in sight red, so bright,
Next dashes in sight green, so light.

Leaves freshly green, dancing in grace,
Fleet, against green red doesn't race.
Begonia goes through nights of rains,
While alive, she stands fine through pains.

鹧鸪天（其十三）

涧水粼粼苍翠中，
芦林湖畔绿葱茏。
含鄱吐日云携雾，
五老听泉玉障笼。

杉柏碧，老梧桐，
千枝蔓起挂蝶虫。
层峦叠嶂青一色，
清涧蜿蜒碧几泓。

A Partridge in the Sky (No. 13)

The stream water is clear, the forest vast;
All around the Lulin Lake green is cast,
Hanpo Pass seen with cloud 'nd fog hand in hand,
Five Old Men Peak greened by some magic wand.

Firs 'nd cypress green, phoenix trees old,
To the interlacing branches worms mold.
Behold, layers upon layers of green!
Creeks wind a few ways out a greatest scene.

春 风

春风料峭柳梢头，
恋恋冬花几簇留。
梅朵依依零散落，
新枝缱绻摆轻柔。

The Spring Wind

The chill wind of spring touches the branch end;
A few winter flowers resist the trend.
At an interval, down plum blossoms twirl,
As budding twigs in the air sway and swirl.

不相愁

时光荏苒染白头，
念念苍苍往岁秋。
惚恍经年人已老，
陈年旧事不相愁。

Let Old Pages Turned

Hair painted white by time that's gone long past,
For the duration time raced by so fast.
It seems that I have been old for ages,
In which what happened has been turned pages.

垂 柳

新芽抽穗柳依依，
一沐春阳垂摆低。
料峭东风枝曼舞，
文波动影伴鸣啼。

The Weeping Willow

In winds the budding willows sway around,
Which droop in the sun almost to the ground.
The east wind blows fine branches to dance, chill;
With birds' chirps, their shadows romp in the rill.

春 树

绿镶堤柳碧成行，
新玉环渠楚水长。
袅袅轻枝摇翡翠，
千株万树若隋唐。

Spring Trees

Willows along the bank, a greenish train,
New-born green lines the river, viewed in vain.
In the spring breeze sway and strain twigs and leaves,
Myriads of them like under old times' eaves.

扬州四月

扬州值四月，
姹紫艳红时。
柳絮飘烟雨，
春来百日熙。

The April of Yangzhou

In April is Yangzhou,
Purples and reds on show,
In catkins flying time,
The sunshine's in its prime.

海棠怒放

春之晨

春晨闻鸟语，
举岸续花香。
一缕清风去，
红衣也挽芳。

A Spring Morning

Bird in the morning heard to sing,
Both of the banks scented of spring.
A whiff of aroma goes by;
On even clothes it does lie.

看图言春

春风斜细柳，
玄鸟自南归。
江水山重秀，
百花次第追。

A Picture of Spring

Spring wind slants wickers of th' willow.
From the south back home comes th' swallow.
Rills mirror hills as the range goes.
Flowers come out rows upon rows.

春 深

浅清着色映丹心，
倩影纤纤待唱吟。
春愈深深辄随遇，
指间流淌懿光阴。

In the Depth of Spring

Spring colors, light and clear, cheer me,
Delightful as chanted to be.
Deep spring is set in what you see;
Good time flows allowing no plea.

杜鹃花开

空庭人愈醒，
瑟瑟扰催眠。
窗下花飞雨，
幽幽伴杜鹃。

The Azaleas in Bloom

With no one around, I can't sleep;
Rustles of wind tell the night's deep.
Outside is th' whirling petal rain,
With azaleas just by the pane.

春 夜

夜来华落雨，
风过响竹林。
花溅池清处，
春深与共吟！

A Spring Night

Onto the ground the night blooms crash.

The bamboo grove rustles with th' breeze.

Into the pond the petals splash.

All this comes to a poem of ease.

琼　花

兰蔻玉华夫，
春深朵朵出。
河中徐漫步，
花绽万千株。

The Jade Flower

The flower is but a white jade,

Coming out, while spring has been late.

I walk th' bank with a leisure gait;

My view blossoming ones invade.

长相思（其一）

白杜鹃，

粉杜鹃，

春雨涟涟人好眠，

梦中花语千？

大雨连，

细雨连，

花落纷纷谁竞嫣？

唯缘桃李先。

Long Longing (No. 1)

White Azalea,

Pink Azalea,

With drizzles on, men sleep just right.

My dream's a garden site.

The heavy rain,

The light, light rain,

Why do those flowers fall a ton?

'Cause they have first begun.

长相思（其二）

青枇杷，
黄枇杷，
小院渠汀竟盛发，
岸帷人几家？

绿枇杷，
金枇杷，
对面庭园寻细芽，
不虞枝缀霞。

Long Longing (No. 2)

Green ones,
Ripe ones,
The loquat on the tree becomes untold.
Around many houses unfold.

Green ones,
Golden ones,
In the opposite garden, we find spring.
The twigs in the glow it does bring!

长相思（其三）

一树芽，
两树芽，
燕过浮萍栖枝丫，
丫间落几葩。

一树花，
两树花，
绿粉菁菁若绮纱，
株株桃杏华。

Long Longing (No. 3)

A tree of buds,

Two trees of buds,

Swallows skim over duckweed up to th' tree;

There lie flowers one can just see.

A tree of blooms,

Two trees of blooms.

Red blooms and green leaves gauzelike spring does reach:

Blossoms of apricot and peach.

长相思（其四）

东风清，
西风清，
风过枝头吹落英。
几重红满庭。

南风清，
北风清，
聒碎秋愁谁愿听。
盈盈独立行。

Long Longing (No. 4)

The eastward wind,
The westward wind,
As the winds pass, fallen flowers abound;
Layers of th' fallen strew the ground.

The southward wind,
The northward wind,
My trifles, can I share with any one?
About them all, I talk to none.

长相思（其五）

城之茵，
水之茵，
杨柳蓁蓁碧长芩，
离离原上心。

天上寻，
水上寻，
那是十八陈令君，
空灵秀若云。

Long Longing (No. 5)

The city green,
The water green,
The poplar 'nd the willow lush and serene,
Her figure's fine and clean.

A heaven scene,
A river scene,
It's a photo of Lingjun at eighteen.
Fairylike she has been.

长相思（其六）

风一更，
雨一更，
四月听闻风雨声，
临别天欲晴。

山一程，
水一程，
身向扬州那畔行，
长思自苑亭。

Long Longing (No. 6)

Breeze of hours ,
Rain of hours,
We've had four months' clamour of wind and rain,
When we leave, the sunshine to gain.

A range of hills,
A belt of rills,
On our trip to th' land of Yangzhou are we.
For long, at home we've longed to be.

长相思（其七）

盛一程，
寥一程，
古尽悠悠人可能。
道其无可争。

此相逢，
彼相逢，
九水枯时仍有棱。
但说喜此生。

Long Longing (No. 7)

Honored,
Humbled,
From of old, what one can't is NOT.
Whatever it is is to rot.

Apart,
Around,
Have the edge till the rills run dry.
Make your life of joy, not a sigh.

深 径

清幽帏绿寂，
深径景输黎。
郁郁诗中语，
风来使更怡。

Deep Along the Trail

Curtained, remote, green, and serene,
Deep along the trail: quite a scene.
As refined words in the poem go,
A little wind betters it so.

春 曲

摇曳葱葱百木枝，
伶仃独作静娴痴。
芳泽宇下谁息处，
春曲缠缠百句诗。

The Spring Tune

Trees sway and strain in the wind green;
I compose, focused and alone.
Whose home is it somewhere unseen?
Spring lingers: a poetic tone.

忆江南（其一）

扬州好，

美景缀彤颜。

戴粉香襟栖绿卷，

兰香扑面粉红怜。

怎不意绵绵？

The South of the River to Mind (No. 1)

Yangzhou is fair;

On good scenes she's intent.

Just over the green is pink and red glare;

Straight to the nose is the natural scent.

Won't you long to be there?

忆江南（其二）

扬州雨，
绵降褪红颜。
卸粉钗红惜绿意，
连连霖曲眷心闲，
独恋北江南。

The South of the River to Mind (No. 2)

The rain drops pound,
Beating the spring flower aground.
Red and pink gone, green fits on the surround;
The rain non-stop, such leisure comes around.
Nowhere else can the scene be found.

忆江南(其三)

扬州雨，

一月数连天。

未到枝头梅紫季，

千滴雨下打书轩。

独悦彼沾沾。

The South of the River to Mind (No. 3)

Here it has rained,

For most days in a moon.

When green red bayberries remained,

When the raindrops beat my cocoon,

I'm glad for what's attained.

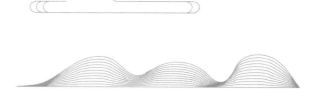

忆江南（其四）

江南雨，

四月欲绵绵。

最爱依栏独赏绿，

蒙蒙碧翠雨如烟。

似汝泪涟涟。

The South of the River to Mind (No. 4)

On th' rain I'm keen,

Though rainy April seems an aeon.

I'm fond of, by the rail, watching the green.

The rain makes, mist over the lush, a scene!

A morose lady she has been!

忆江南（其五）

扬州好，
春景尽葳蕤。
围傍勤思天下似，
藉词不问世间非。
谁道此无为？

The South of the River to Mind (No. 5)

Yangzhou does sheen.
Where spring comes with eyefuls of green.
By the rail, one ponders what life does mean;
With the poem, one stops thinking of the woe.
Who would say fruitless he would go?

忆江南（其六）

扬州好，
风景旧婵娟。
夏日风吹环绿柳，
三秋雨打起濛烟，
窗外杳凭栏。

The South of the River to Mind (No. 6)

Good is Yangzhou,
Fair still is the old Yangzhou scene!
Summer winds whiffle, round willows which go;
Autumn drizzles fall, misty whose view's been.
Out the window is a good show.

忆江南(其七)

扬州忆,

去去是长安。

不问平明嘈盛夏,

但吟今日慰鸣蝉。

只愿总悠然。

The South of the River to Mind (No. 7)

Yangzhou to mind I call,

A wonderful time we had all.

Never ask if tomorrow will be fall;

Just know that today is the summer glee.

Better always be so carefree.

忆江南（其八）

清秋色，
穆穆偶凭栏。
浊乱常如秋百索，
悲愁偶印夏阑珊。
夜里怼寒蝉。

The South of the River to Mind (No. 8)

On a clear autumn sight,
By the window I let calm flow.
As many a thought came, my heart gets tight;
When summer leaves, my spirits remain low;
I blame cicada chirps at night.

忆江南（其九）

扬之色，
一载万千重。
叶生芽发徐晕绿，
箨枯丹落速漆红。
秋到这时浓。

The South of the River to Mind (No. 9)

Yangzhou's hue in no range,

The year sees it on constant change.

Leaves grow and buds appear, slowly all green;

Flowers fall and leaves go red: a great scene.

Lo, the depths of autumn it's been!

忆江南(其十)

萧萧木，
秋叶落缤疾。
红染丛丛当孕秀，
鹭白对对落长堤。
来日哪堪题！

The South of the River to Mind (No. 10)

Off the trees is the green;

Leaves fall rustling at a fast pace.

Red in dyed clusters, making a great scene;

Egrets in pairs, perching on th' bank with grace.

The future is not unforeseen!

忆江南（其十一）

登高处，
一丈绿青葱。
遥想少年身郁暗，
尤怀愁绪心明红。
秋去已隆冬。

The South of the River to Mind (No. 11)

Climbing to a great height,
I see a vast expanse of green.
Taken to mind is the youngster's old sight;
Taken to heart is th' future to be seen.
In winter, my way forth I fight.

点绛唇

鸣鸟喧嘈，
轩栏窗里无觉扰。
赋文唯好。
不问闲人早。

拆髻梳鬟，
独作容颜老。
熟难料。
立之还照，
对镜痴痴笑。

Rouged Lips

Birds' chatters and chirps din,
While focused and undisturbed one has been.
Writing poems just for fun,
She says Good Morning but to none.

Combing her long black hair,
She looks years older in the casual wear.
This who would bear?
Seeing th' mirror again,
She laughs, which goes beyond your ken.

蝶恋花

春韵生愉园树迚，
亭槛栏轩，
人欲翩翩逗。
偏爱千花唇欲就？
重吟百句眉方皱。

鸟语诉衷吟碧凑，
不见繁华，
历历菁菁秀。
但恋扬州滋豆蔻，
唯怜垂柳题春瘦。

The Butterfly in Love with Blooms

Encountered are blossoms on trees of spring.
A recessed garden scene!
For me to stay, my heart on th' wing,
On nothing but the flower I am keen;
Of nothing but sad poems I am to sing.

Birds' chirps chant out my heart on the new green.
Gone, flowers have a fling.
A riot of them: quite a sheen!
I love but Yangzhou with seedlings to bring.
The weeping willows never make spring lean.

扬州之春

绿嫩枝丫几度回，
满园郁郁斗芳菲。
几颗俏紫梢上簇，
柳絮杨花草长肥。

The Spring of Yangzhou

Tender twigs have shot a tenth time,
When green plants blossom in their prime.
On treetops cluster purple buds;
Grass grows greener and catkins flood.

浣溪沙（其一）

款款秋冬暮恋曦，
秋迟老叶篝成衣。
离离碧草赋虞姬。

眺览层层尘挡目，
喧鸣婉婉乐成机，
惚惚恍恍梦须臾。

Yarn Washing (No. 1)

On short days for autumn 'nd winter to meet,
Old yellowish leaves coat the tree for heat;
Dreamlike grass remains green and lush, so sweet.

Through a mist of dust where one's eyes arrive,
Birds' cheerful chatters bring the banks to thrive;
Out of a moment's sleep one comes alive.

浣溪沙（其二）

碧草携金玉样葱，
红梅渐盛玉湖同，
如兰楚水擅玲珑？

婉婉彤彤托暮色，
粼粼淼淼荡春红，
离离翠碧欲荫浓。

Yarn Washing (No. 2)

Starred with a trace of gold is th' grassy green;
The plum blossoms go furious: quite a scene.
The greenish water's delicate with sheen.

It glints in response with the twilight gold.
Ripples of th' river: a story spring's told.
Leafy trees: a spring picture to unfold.

浣溪沙（其三）

初雪银装碧木荒，
蒹葭冰冻水粮藏，
少年一去已成乡。

无可奈何冬落霜，
似曾相仿邂春芳，
丹心一片莫彷徨。

Yarn Washing (No. 3)

Gone in the town, th' first snow sees trees snow-capped,
Reeds dry and frozen with the earth snow-wrapped,
I left my hometown young after I packed.

With the frost in winter, do what one may;
Met somewhere before, sweet scents in spring spray;
Take the here as my hometown not to sway.

探 春

嫩细吐三春，
水波荡绿深。
堤围初染翠，
旧去了无痕。

Tracing Spring

Tender green springs up on the tree.
Leaves greener, waves leap forth with glee.
The banks just get dressing in green,
Away the bygone age has been.

乡 晨

啾啾鸣闹贯长空，
高耀晨阳画上红。
香入心脾春醉梦，
黄花朵朵灿微浓。

Morning in the Countryside

Birds' chirps across the air from far away,
The mid-morning pictured with the sun spray,
The soul-delighting scent brings a sweet dream;
The yellow rape flowers give out a gleam.

桃花（其一）

桃花十里竞红芳，
柳绿青青可哪藏？
不负灼灼不负己，
残华未悯莫怜殇。

The Peach Blossom (No. 1)

The peach blossoms in a train come to vie;
Willows leaves green, how does spring shun the eye?
Live up to the shining blooms and myself;
For withered blossoms in sight, never sigh.

桃花（其二）

粉琢千万染重重，
堤上嫣然映照红。
看淡人间多变色，
汤汤花溢正春浓。

The Peach Blossom (No. 2)

Hued in pinks of many a shade,
A long train the peach trees have made.
The peach blooms outshines all curious;
Spring in th' air is going furious.

四月桃花

灼灼潋滟几多赋，
难话其实点点妖。
四月未歇花但落，
长堤十里坠青桃。

The Peach Blossom in April

The peach blossom shines in rhyme after rhyme;
It's difficult to depict all its prime.
Up to May it is unable to reach,
On the long bank patrol trees with the peach.

春 发

春风得劲绿低洼，
万树千丛处处芽。
苇草当发寒欲去，
馨芳送暖趣闲暇。

The Beginning of Spring

As spring wind blows, green is a flood.

Everywhere myriads of trees bud.

Grass grows, seeing cold off the mud,

Warmth with sweet scent sends spring to th' blood.

闲 适

蜿蜒曲水赴天边，
楚水玲珑九道弯。
欲捕鸬鹚空自坐，
鹅鸭曲项锁窗闲。

A Leisure Scene

The river romps to the end of the earth,
Winding its zigzag way nicely with mirth.
In the canoe cormorants wait to hunt,
Geese looking up: a leisure scene in front!

檀香山之雨

连日绵绵雨，
滴滴意采渠。
滋高原上草，
四季莫将枯。

The Rain of Honolulu

Rain, rain, many a day,
Leaves puddles on the way,
Watering grass in th' hill;
Four seasons see no hay.

檀香山之春

栖逗长青地，
光阴溢满春。
浮云天蔚碧，
放眼异族人。

The Spring of Honolulu

I stay in the evergreen land;
The spring aroma does expand.
Above are clouds and the blue sky;
People of all colours come nigh.

春 迹

徐徐纹水漾河堤，
垂柳依依碧叶栖。
两岸葱葱昔日树，
无踪旧迹满怀疑。

Seeking the Trail of Spring

Water ripples to the banks in light wind;
On weeping willows leaves are newly pinned.
The trees are as lush as they were last year;
I wonder why the trail of spring's gone here.

荷 塘

荷塘月色扬州邑，
藕断丝牵恋不移。
也有别乡曾泪泣，
湖边明月照无极。

The Lotus Pond

Th' lotus pond in Yangzhou the moon does light;
The tie between the pond and me is tight.
Crying with sobs, to the west I did wend;
The bright moon lit the land to not an end.

花　殇

花美留行客，
繁华竟落殇。
春花一朵朵，
哪朵断柔肠！

On Fallen Flowers

The flowers engage passers-by,
Who sighs for flowers that die young?
Blooms upon blooms come to the eye;
To the soul which on earth has sprung?

春 去

繁英绛去间，
恍若瞬息然。
密绿春华落，
终归翠木凡！

Spring Going Away

Dark red flowers suffer a fall,
Which happened in no time at all.
Amid green trees, spring blooms are gone:
A common scene with green leaves on.

入 夏

清露湖边依傍水，
缤纷落去渐春阑。
夜初入夏蛙声远，
幕下荷塘未见莲。

Beginning of Summer

In and around the water was the bloom;
Flowers fall and to an end is th' spring boom,
Few frog-croaks on the early summer night,
The lotus at the water-level height.

青荷白鹭

青青浅叶纤荷田，
仨俩划空若小仙。
一亩幽莲方露水，
春雏化鹭上九天。

The Lotus and the Egret

Clean, vast, and green-leafed, a lotus patch lies;
Egrets skim past, like fairies in the skies.
An expanse of lotuses first on show,
Chicks into egrets, up to th' sky they go.

雨

夏尝噲雨夜汀淹，
围翠长堤沐水眠。
欲打陈联低玉燕，
茫茫延展径蜿蜒。

The Rain

Flooded by the summer rains in a row,

The green-lined banks lie in the rain below.

It strikes couplets off and swallows fly low;

The path winds down and forward it does go.

不 怨

一室欣欣满室兰，
时光流逝忆从前。
余愁销去犹遗惋，
不怨芳华顷刻间。

No Grief

The whole house filled with cheery solar rays,
As time flies, I recall the good old days.
With a little comfort, least regret though,
I am happy to have had my youth glow.

游庐山

登台望去幽悠莛，
古树千帘枝蔓菁。
娟宛溪流依嶂舞，
幽泉汩汩趣石清。

A Tour of Mount Lushan

Seen from high is all stunning green,
Limbs of old trees knit into th' screen.
Spring water runs over stones clean;
Cheerily down th' mountain it's been.

夏

谢却嫩芽飞尽絮，
枝头栖处是黄莺。
紫团簇簇侵葱绿，
夏日清清看紫荆。

Summer

Catkins fall off, buds going big.
An oriole perches on the twig.
Purple flowers cluster in green;
Bauhinia is the summer scene.

思

灼灼明艳绽春妍，
桃色须臾落影怜。
柳絮乘风方与醉，
万千思绪忆流年。

My Thought

In the time of spring the peach blossoms shine.
Before they fall, a short time they are fine.
Catkins in the wind make me dream and pine
A great deal for the good old years of mine.

踏莎行

初夏春阑，
葳蕤碧杳。
清屏落艳芳菲少。
离离幽径踏一程，
徜徉朗朗读青草。

日去西沉，
余晴尚好。
琼花仍在枝繁茂。
红尘无语竟销魂，
苍天若许徐徐老。

Treading on Grass

Early summer ere spring,
For the vast green we sing.
Petals going fallen, flowers are few;
The path remains lush, which is a good view.
For more plants we find new we stroll in quest.

Climbing down in the west,
The setting sun does shine.
The jade flower remain in bloom, leaves fine.
The world is no way perfect, but a thrill,
If God allows, time flows past at my will.

葳蕤生花

葳蕤如梦坠青葱，
簇簇伸延巧俏重。
杳展枝头调彩色，
轩窗斜坠扮丹红。

The Bracketplant in Bloom

The flowerlets hang from the flower pot,
Pretty in clusters when th' weather gets hot,
Blooms multi-hued at the tip of the vine,
Which are leaning against the window, fine.

春余婷

春时香袅袅，
夏至蜜枇青。
夜色销魂处，
夏初溢芳婷。

Spring Spill in Early Summer

In spring, sweet the air scent has been;
As summer comes loquats stay green.
In the night, what triggers a thrill?
Early summer sees spring air spill.

天净沙（其一）

薄雾缈缈凉凉，
远兮悠袤苍苍。
碧海无垠翠染。
山溪喧下，
不知踪迹行藏。

Sand in the Sun (No. 1)

Gauze misty with a chill,
Mount and dale green does fill,
Boundless, an oxygen mill.
Down th' creek does trill;
It's out of sight at will.

天净沙（其二）

伏蛰静室兰心，
正平七月时阴。
勿惑时光尽好。
从容隔世，
履及盛夏禅音。

Sand in the Sun (No. 2)

With my mind little rippled and peaceful,
Though it's oft cloudy, July's wonderful.
No wonder it is good time as usual.
Attempting not to be social,
I roam for best sounds imaginable.

天净沙（其三）

薇丛碧树黄花，
大鸿白鹭人家。
恋就天边那染。
薄云赤水，
醉收一幕残霞。

Sand in the Sun (No. 3)

Green trees and daisies and the rest;
Wild geese and egrets and the nest.
What in the world is loved the best?
Gold cloud 'nd water in quest:
A waning glow scene is so blessed.

天净沙（其四）

祥云白鹭蓝天，
九花金桂人间。
小径清风送晚。
兰亭别苑，
最玲珑似从前。

Sand in the Sun (No. 4)

Auspicious clouds and egrets in the sky,
Chrysanthemum and osmanthus on earth,
In the breeze, evening stalks up along th' trail.
Pavilions 'nd mansions fail
To age in every fine detail.

天净沙（其五）

青天绿水红霞，
损竹枯叶黄花。
白鹭一行入景。
葱葱小院，
影孤思念无他。

Sand in the Sun (No. 5)

Th' blue sky, green water, and th' sun's evening glow!
Sheaths of bamboo, dead leaves and blooms that grow!
In sight comes a flock of egrets in line.
With the garden on th' vine,
I think of no other affairs of mine.

天净沙（其六）

一枝两杈黄梅，
对空如欲双飞。
几朵娇颜绽放。
花拥簇簇，
似说冬去还回。

Sand in the Sun (No. 6)

A forky twig is found in pair,
Which seeks to pair-fly in the air.
Several plum blossoms in full bloom,
Clusters of them to boom,
They say goes and comes winter gloom.

天净沙（其七）

茫茫雾霭重重，
匆匆八野空空。
几日容颜骤绽。
葱茏聚散，
此为中楚之冬。

Sand in the Sun (No. 7)

The mistiness goes vast;
The sunshine goes off fast.
When did the sun here last?
The lush gone past,
So is winter here cast.

天净沙（其八）

残黄桂淡梅从，
瓣红苞染冬隆。
退却秋枝杳绿。
枯荣序展，
此时寒意才浓。

Sand in the Sun (No. 8)

To plum blossoms yellow flowers retreat;
Th' depth of winter red petals and buds meet.
The green of autumn in the distance goes.
The plant withers and grows,
At which time, the dead of winter just shows.

千 岛

蒙蒙雨烟染梅红，
屿岛难寻百里东。
谁撒千珠湖水上，
丹青水墨画觉浓。

A Thousand Islets

The rain mist helps tint the bayberries red;
To the west it's hard to find th' islet bed.
Who's scattered a thousand pearls in the lake?
Like paintings the scenery's but not fake.

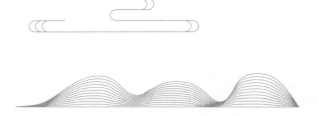

仲夏之夜

月洒灰云上，
深更仲夏长。
蛙声一阵远，
吟凑己彷徨。

A Mid-summer Night

The moon through clouds gives a veiled light;
Th' mid-summer has a longer night.
A burst of croaks sounds far away;
A lady chants her idled day.

思 乡

秋来愈是慨离殇，
最是门前桂满香。
去去曈昽携旭日，
今朝梦里见潇湘。

Homesickness

Fall brings a separation sigh;
At the door th' osmanthus grows nigh.
The sunny days of the past year,
I dream tonight about with tears.

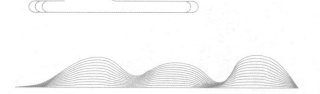

秋 意

凉风清夏意，
秋至噪微低。
午后来袭热，
知鸣渐度歇。

Autumn in the Air

Cool air clears the summer away;
Cicadas' din sounds not that gay.
Afternoon heat comes as before;
Their merry chirps are not in store.

秋 风

秋风挽发丝，
枯落百千枝。
粉黛青犹在，
青丝逗几时？

Autumn Wind

Coiled up in autumn breezy air,
In hundreds falls my dear long hair.
The lady's black hair remains though;
Off the colour's destined to go.

秋 色

秋至天高远，
云积日半藏。
金辉承瑞气，
常道几沧桑。

Autumn Hue

As autumn comes, the sky looks far;
To the sunlight the cloud's a bar.
The golden glow bears the good sign;
A life of changes is yours 'nd mine.

一剪梅

秋意初来夏日当，
一亩荷塘，
缕缕莲香。
春生暑长藕方长，
两瓣清芳，
未断丝浆。

此去来时秋愈凉，
夜半才刚，
久梦茫茫。
更深尤恋彼时扬，
月下吟殇，
心自彷徨。

A Spray of Plum Blossoms

The broiling sun stays up with autumn air,
A vast lotus field rare,
From which comes the sweet scent.
Spring and summer, its grown ripe root has spent.
Sweetness out of th' cut one,
Th' fibers stringed, off is none.

From now on, cooler goes the autumn night.
Just in th' middle of night,
My long dreams go unbound.
At midnight, th' love's more for what's then around.
Chanted for under th' moon,
My heart does pace and croon.

青 莲

青莲待饰散花香，
初绽含羞衣绿裳。
秋溢浓浓托夜色，
酣然入梦见荷塘。

The Lotus

The young lotus, light-scented, waits to bloom,
Half open, shy-looking, attired in green.
The autumn spill brings the night chill to loom;
In one's sound sleep the lotus pond is seen.

秋 丝

青丝落万千，
理乱断秋难。
固发青丝少，
花白不只三。

The Loss of Good Hair

Black hair's fallen a lot.
In autumn it's much shed.
Less and less black hair's got?
The grey's left on the head.

秋（其一）

只影凭栏一盏酒，
风来花落又说秋。
那年孤对他乡月，
曾几悲忧欲愈愁？

Autumn (No. 1)

Alone by the rail, with a cup of wine,

As wind blows, flowers dead: autumn of mine.

Alien, she was lonely under the moon.

Over woe she was liable to swoon.

秋（其二）

恨遇秋来菡百残，
天高偶见燕低檐。
长堤洼地寻白鹭，
常望一行上碧天。

Autumn(No. 2)

Not many a lotus autumn receives;
Flying high, birds sometimes perch under eaves.
Egrets live in the wetlands of Yangzhou,
Often observed in the sky in a row.

秋（其三）

淅淅吹落叶斑斑，
凉水潺潺雨亦娟。
不为落红薄夏色，
秋妍楚楚雅如兰。

Autumn (No. 3)

The wind rustles off leaves, mottled aground;
Flows in the rain give a beautiful sound.
The summer scene stays though flowers wither;
Fine and fair, the autumn view does abound.

秋（其四）

清灵日远挽凉居，
枯叶纷纷落入溪。
一树桂花枝满郁，
西亭内外尽秋栖。

Autumn (No. 4)

The weather cold, the sun is going far;
Withered leaves come non-stop down in the stream.
So fragrant the osmanthus flowers are;
With th' autumn feel the neighborhood does teem.

秋（其五）

皓霞婉影但知凉，
白露成霜秋月藏。
天色舒蓝悠渡远，
琼瑶万里鹭一行。

Autumn (No. 5)

The bright moon shines, graceful but cold;
It's sometimes nowhere to behold.
Into the cleared and farther sky,
In a single file, egrets fly.

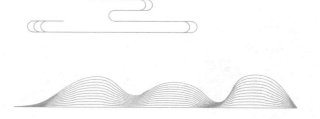

秋（其六）

秋涛河瘦漾涟漪，
绿黛映青曲水西。
素染葱葱蓝若玉，
乾坤朗朗醉渠堤。

Autumn (No. 6)

Autumn winds soften the stiff river best;
All the shaded green there is to its west.
The trees remain lush, the river blue blue;
Under the clear sky, everything's so true.

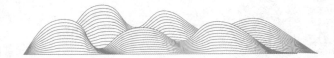

秋（其七）

昨夜听风归已晚，
稀疏百寐遇秋残。
冷风为伴艳红去，
叶落萧萧莽溢寒。

Autumn (No. 7)

I did come home late on a windy night,
Sleep broken some times to the season sight.
Th' golden leaves the chill autumn wind blew off;
The fall of leaves came from the nature's might.

秋（其八）

枫木初红碧露微，
背依蓝幕叶徐飞。
白霜愈点金秋色，
待去纷纷落几枚。

Autumn (No. 8)

Maple leaves drift, reddish with little dew;
Against the blue screen, they are falling slow.
The frost lights the vast earth golden anew,
Few upon few, the leaves fall in a row.

忆王孙

葳蕤如静绿随醺，
翠黛翩翩微染裙。
燕转朱阁兀自矜，
梦中君，
雾霭茫茫秋使氲。

A Recollection of My Friend

Dangling still, the green renders me tipsy,
Dancing lightly, it renders me merry.
Birds fly from this house to th' next while I stay;
So dreamy in a way,
The earth turns misty on the autumn day.

秋 雨

潇潇绵雨打屋檐，
落叶归根广宇前。
白昼枯颜长宿夜，
悠悠楚水入溪潭。

Autumn Rain

The autumn rain patters onto the eaves;
Onto the vast ground are the fallen leaves.
Bleak by day with the prolonged rain by night,
The river streams somewhere no one receives.

又 见

斜阳渐去水微低，
残影青红映水西。
潜邸几出昔日去，
时光荏苒莫须急。

Encounter Made Again

Into the water the sunlight slants low,
Plants reflected to the west in the flow.
Some buildings towering over the past,
Time would better linger and not go fast.

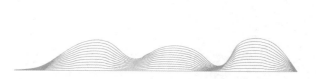

中秋桂香

月寂挂长空，
难遮桂树红。
幽香千百里，
风过至江东。

Sweet Scent of Mid-autumn

The light of the lonely moon flows
Upon osmanthus in full bloom.
Across miles and miles her scent blows
Through the wind even to the room.

浪淘沙

秋意到来难，
夜裹衾单。
犹思往日寐当年。
不问宵深多段梦，
梦里嫣然。

独自偶凭栏，
事与谁谈。
将别恨怨喜豪言。
不枉经时人渐醒，
何处而安。

Waves Washing Sand

Autumn is struggling here;
I'm using the quilt light.
The past to mind, I dream of th' bygone year.
Don't mind how many dreams to have a night,
Which causes me to cheer.

On occasion against the pane,
With whom the pain to share,
To get out of this, myself to regain,
Of the past sadness of mine, I'm aware.
Where am I to stretch 'nd strain?

初 雪

纷纷洒落三千尺，
一阵疾风卷载烟。
漫漫依依栖赤叶，
玉红片片雪织帘。

First Snow

Snow falls from heaven, dancing it way down;
It fumes and swirls as a gust of wind blows.
It perches on the leaves that are bright brown;
But like red jade, coated in snow they go.

冬（其一）

清晨入目土尘扬，
日照高楼万缕光。
鸟雀啁啾人耳后，
树梢丹桂几时黄？

Winter (No. 1)

In the morn, to the dirt one is not blind;
The building hugs the sunshine to its breast.
While sparrows let out chatters just behind,
When in yellow osmanthus will be dressed?

冬（其二）

冬来袅袅送秋徐，
落叶霏霏雨雪疏。
凛凛窗寒霖欲霁，
飞黄红絮只须臾。

Winter (No. 2)

This year winter is coming slow;
Fallen leaves swirl down without snow.
The chill rain has surpassed its prime;
Th' season shift takes just a short time.

冬（其三）

濛濛烟雨落渠堤，
冬景无言却作题。
无处寻菊独悦目，
公孙树下未秋离。

Winter (No. 3)

A mist of rain falls down into the rill;
The dull scene brings forth no poetic thrill.
Hardly found somewhere is the winter hint;
Heavy is the under-tree autumn tint.

冬（其四）

秋影重重竟已冬，
寒居几日却憧憧。
日出狷介和而泰，
土硬春藏且走觥。

Winter (No. 4)

Short autumn doesn't stand the winter pull;
It's cold a few days with a golden foil.
The sun is up, its light mild to the full;
Soil hardens for spring where you do not toil.

冬（其五）

三竿冬日使微醺，
正冷当时总盼春。
无奈苍穹盛碧色，
蒙蒙旖旎似霞赟。

Winter (No. 5)

Captivating, the winter sun does rise.
It being cold, I hope for spring to th' eyes,
Only that under the sky is all green,
As great as the evening glow, a fine scene.

腊梅（其一）

寒冬腊月愈浇漓，
敛色梅香一段奇。
绮丽婀娜冬映色，
妍于百里遂妖姬。

The Wintersweet (No. 1)

During the coldest time of the twelfth moon,
Retaining hues, she is just smelling sweet.
Pretty and graceful, she blossoms in tune,
So fine a thing that nothing else can beat.

腊梅（其二）

梅发元月早，
二月树千花。
万秀红山屿，
初春最看她。

The Wintersweet (No. 2)

The wintersweet buds in the coldest time;
In the second month she is in her prime.
Ten thousand trees adorn the winter hill;
In the early spring, its beauty does spill.

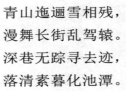

雪

青山逶迤雪相残，
漫舞长街乱驾辕。
深巷无踪寻去迹，
落清素暮化池潭。

The Snow

The greenish hills witness the waning snow
That inconveniences the traffic so.
The alley is not snowy any more;
The melting on its own saves up the chore.

临江仙（其一）

日暮暗汀寻月影，

风消聊赖清修。

垂杨舞柳映帆舟，

蓦然回首处，

几幕是扬州。

碧水蓝庭如缟素，

雨淋寥寂空收？

随心淡欲寡闲愁，

落红说夙怨，

百缕上心头。

Celestial Beings by the River (No. 1)

At evening I look forward to the moon;

I'm carefree, finding it a boon.

Where poplars and willows dance along th' trail,

When I call to mind the old tale,

My mind on Yangzhou is all true.

The water is green under the sky blue;

In solitude out of the rain,

I am joyful with no worry or pain.

Sorry for the petals aground,

I find my tender self grief-bound.

临江仙（其二）

夏仲喧阑西苑静，
倚窗听寂寻空。
丽华才遇绮罗穷。
朱楼歌散去，
轻调已无踪。

日月不识颜色改，
苍天独眷池中？
粉香菡萏暮中红。
更深风碎梦，
岁月尽朦胧。

Celestial Beings by the River (No. 2)

My dwelling place tranquil without a breeze,
I try to have my mind at ease.
In the deepest of the mid-summer night,
With songs gone, there'd be something trite.
Gone, yesterday was holy blessed.

Only I know that the days were my best;
God loves the lotus in the pond?
Every summer it'd be another blonde.
A sudden breeze clears up my mind:
The old days were all left behind.

临江仙（其三）

风打绮窗酣梦醒，
清幽愁怼随风。
韶华一曲劲匆匆。
挽江南绿影，
风骤景千重。

霞映苍苍托皓月，
夜阑还照深丛。
婷婷袅袅越河东。
莫伤菁翠去，
淡淡杏香浓。

Celestial Beings by the River (No. 3)

Awakened by a gust of savage wind,
I complained, but away it shinned.
Like the spring blossom, youth has gone too soon.
At th' night scene of the South I swoon;
Wind rises: a charming night scene.

With hued clouds around, out of the moon sheen,
Moonlight flows to th' deep of the bush,
Across the river for a further push.
Let the bygone age gone;
See what is going on.

临江仙（其四）

红叶黄花何处是？
徐徐细雨扬扬。
离离葱木楚萦桑。
谓其今属楚，
颦蹙泪千行。

崇最潇潇绵雨后，
教人愈怕冬长。
谁能未感夜凄凉。
恍惚多少梦，
为百绪衷藏。

Celestial Beings by the River (No. 4)

Maple leaves and gold flowers found nowhere,
Only drizzles rustle in th' air.
The lush green bears a large share of the here.
With some unabiding good cheer,
Brows knit, I meditate on something dear.

Fond of the scene after the constant rain,
I'm afraid winter will remain,
And whoever won't feel th' night's freezing pain.
With beans the chamber mill is filled;
They are not going to be spilled.

临江仙（其五）

楚水冬凉残去了，
独尝一刻夕阳。
葱葱芊木溢彐裳。
明明寻日影，
恍恍步徜徉。

云雀啁啾别式样，
可曾讥笑冬藏？
沁脾淡淡桂花香。
闻黄金满树，
怜季季秋殇。

Celestial Beings by the River (No. 5)

While the river water here has run cold,
I alone enjoyed th' setting sun.
Th' luxuriantly green of trees did unfold.
In seeking the sun I had fun;
Stepping on my shadow, I strolled.

The sparrows chattered in a differed tongue;
Was that to mock the fat I hold?
The light-sweet scent stealing into the lung,
Seeing the tree hanging in gold,
I can't but sigh for autumn that died young.

临江仙（其六）

沥沥潇潇昨日雨，
淅淅落去皆无。
苍苍千木叶刚枯。
楚冬银入宿，
一展画弗如。

三季承合镶幕里，
此间离乱微服。
年年岁岁品当初。
春秋多少景，
看尽宛如图。

Celestial Beings by the River (No. 6)

Yesterday's continuous whistling rain,
Drop by drop, falls down aground, gone.
Leaves on many trees are starting to drain.
The winter here sees white put on;
A picture can compare in vain.

Three seasons one after one set in th' scene,
In th' scene are a riot of hues.
From year to year I cherish th' first-met green.
In spring and fall, how many views?
Seen around, a picture it's been.

心 舒

清风抚袖来，
一缕绽心开。
举目一千里，
尘除往日霾。

Feeling Restored

My sleeves are fondled by the breeze
That blows to my heart for a tease.
I look out to a great distance,
Finding th' old bothers gone with ease.

生查子

去年冬就时，
湖畔楼前逗。
日挂柳梢头，
人悦茶余后。

今年冬就时，
湖与楼依旧。
不见去年人，
泪浸冬衣袖。

The Green Haw

As winter just began last year,
Between lake 'nd building we did cheer.
The sun was down over the tree,
When we chattered chuckling in glee.

As winter just begins this year,
The lake and building are still here.
Yet one of us is for good gone;
We wail so for she is that young.

破阵子

窗外葱葱新木，
轩中五彩花株。
夏至暖才八九日，
春到寒还三两出。
絮飞轻劲逐。

拙妇家中恬适，
铲泥翰墨难无。
闲品香茗一角景，
忙作小文几斗斛，
笑生环不如。

The Parade

Outside is an expanse: new green;
Inside are hued plants: a sweet scene.
Summer is just here, but warm days come due;
Spring has been here, but cold visits anew.
Catkins twirl right on cue.

A lady remains fit at home;
With shovel and pen she does roam,
Enjoying the tea and the corner view,
Writing metrical poems quite a few.
Beaming, she's whom I knew.

咏夹竹桃

叶如胡柳郁葱葱，
花比春阳半载红。
雾霭扬尘她哪惧，
携芳吐艳总彤彤！

Ode to the Oleander

The leaf's in shape of willow leaf, lush 'nd green,
Its flowers like the sun, red for an aeon.
She stands there enduring the smog and dirt;
She's always sweet-scented and red, unhurt.

七　绝

凉风耳畔瑟萧疾，
寥寂苍云朵卷低。
新柳沙沙行客晚，
明珠灿灿裹黄衣。

A Quatrain

To my ear, chill wind roars fleetingly by,
Clouds low under the vast expanse of sky.
One's late mid rustles of th' regreened willow;
That's my dearest pearl that glows in yellow.

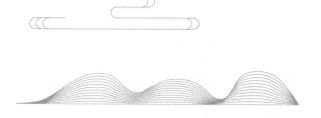

垂 柳

新芽抽穗柳依依，
一沐春阳坠摆低。
料峭东风枝曼舞，
文波动影伴鸣啼。

Weeping Willows

In wind budding willows sway all around;
They droop in the sun almost to the ground.
The chill east wind blows the branches to dance,
Whose shadows with birds' chirps in th' water prance.

七律／墨里寻

残退诗情远至今，
新词成赋告知音。
潇潇夜里一阕醉，
洒洒天中两句吟。
浅叹朦胧浑噩梦，
沉盘清朗玉瑶心。
悠悠岁月悠悠过，
往事潺潺墨里寻。

An Octave/Seeking in Poems

For a while I had no poems, spirits low.
While now a rhyme done, I let my friend know.
Windy nights see me compose a poem part;
Sunny days watch me read it in good heart.
On the confusing dreams a verse or two,
On crystal clear hearts of those, real and true,
I allow time to flow leisurely by:
What is read in each line for me to sigh.

一剪愁

昨日残寒寒入骨，
寥寥漫漫又如秋。
倏然一夜春风暖，
墨里添香一剪愁。

Reduced Woe

Into my bones blows yesterday's spring chill,
Like it's autumn slow slow spring does not fill.
The breezes give rise to warmth overnight;
With woe reduced, joy romps in words so light.

2021 清明

片片黄花万朵低，
春风缕缕瑞芳稀。
清明细雨蒙蒙路，
旧冢新坟众泣啼。

The Tomb Sweeping Day of 2021

Expanses of flowers come in sight low,
As fragrance smells faint, the spring breezes blow.
In drizzles, misty is the country road;
Before old graves and new tombs tears have flowed.

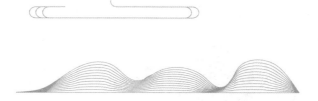

寄　语

骤雨初歇细语低，
喃喃念念梦中啼。
平平淡淡人生路，
款款轻轻莫太急。

To My Daughter

To a whisper abates a sudden rain;

Followed by mumbles and sobs in your sleep.

On the heading-for-future unrough lane,

You needn't rush in anxiety so deep.

晚春游

杳杳苍穹万里空，
午晞溢暖送西风。
轻衫深入林间路，
又见漂流弱水东。

An Outing in the Late Spring

Cloudless, the sky is seen to extend and extend;
A west wind a midday sun warms air up to send.
Deep in to the wood the path leads one girl at least;
To foot a boat a lake invites th' family east.

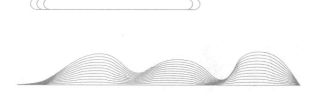

望春（其一）

寒北千花晚，
金梅踏雪来。
冬离春朵盛，
千万紫红开。

Greeting Spring (No. 1)

In th' cold north all flowers late blow;
Plum blossoms come out in the snow.
After winter comes spring in boom;
In spring all flowers vie to bloom.

海棠怒放

望春(其二)

北国寒地花开晚，
凌雪金梅傲放时。
一去隆冬春盛日，
繁华历乱竞相宜。

Greeting Spring (No. 2)

Flowers open late in the north land cold;
Plum blossoms in the snow fully unfold.
When the depth of winter goes, spring does boom;
A riot of flowers vie in full bloom.

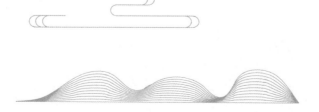

梅雨六月

黄梅节气雨今至，
两日天晴两日阴。
不为明朝空落泪，
昏昏醉梦采禅心。

June of the Plum Rain

To th' present time th' plum season stays,
Sunny two days, cloudy two days.
For th' morrow I don't shed tears blind,
Drowsy like this for peace of mind.

夏 至

翩翩青缕漾池中，
千叶纤花只两红。
浅水微澜轻舞碧，
欲说夏至漫东风。

Summer Solstice

Over the pond flickers the graceful green,
Lily pads many, but two red blooms seen.
Over th' water ripples th' green pads dance fair,
Saying east winds carries the summer air.

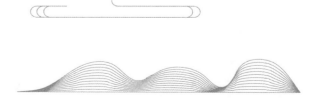

会小秋

同窗三载去悠悠，
解语花为付小秋。
各自前途隔万里，
匆匆一聚在扬州。

Having a Get-together with Xiaoqiu

Gone is the three years when classmates were we;
She was the only one who knew well me;
Far from each other, for our lives we part;
In Yangzhou for two hours, with me thou art.

2022 立春

冬意阑珊处，
春当染色时。
鸟鸣窗外木，
日照户边枝。

The Beginning of Spring in 2022

It's winter's very end;
To the here spring does wend.
Birds chirp out in the pine;
Th' sun shines in on the vine.

望 雪

料峭春方立，
琼瑶雪正飞。
玉英翼路转，
银粟转峰回。

Watching the Snow

Chilly spring just begins;
Precious jade now re-spins.
It wings its way around;
It winds its way aground.

元 夕

寂寂梅香落影疏，
不曾细度有几株。
上元待过清风暖，
生意方来又复苏。

The Lantern Festival

With sweet smell, the wintersweet stands alone;
I never cared how many blooms have grown.
The wind will carry warmth after today;
Life will just come back on its very way.

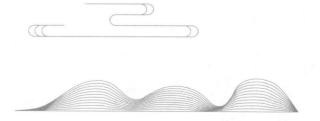

青玉案

东西不问前行路，
总弯转、阑珊处。
千里艰辛风带雨。
华灯初上，
无人声闹，
伏案心无物。

韶华易逝从不驻，
守却元夕此一幕。
莫怕良宵为苦度，
心思暂寄，
玉兰枝上，
明日花开怒！

Green Jade Tray

East or west, not to mind where I would go,
To stop here or there, not to know.
I went through thick and thin, through wind and rain.
Lights have just lit the lane;
No one makes any sound,
Having mind on nothing around.

Without stop the best time of mine has been,
Not to let the Day go, to enjoy th' scene.
Fear not that you will go through the good night.
Where does my mind alight?
Where the magnolias loom,
With their tomorrow's to bloom.

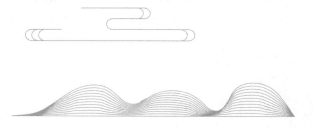

七律/与君约

明月湖边又一环，
临波谈笑黛眉弯。
大江南北红尘似，
内外东西天地闲。
款款并肩移百步，
姗姗对目诉千言。
与君约赴全无宴，
浴沐西风共入禅。

An Octave/A Wonderful Retreat

Round th' Moon Lake, one more lap we walk;
By the lake cheerily we talk.
All trivial matters in the earth,
All current affairs in the earth,
Shoulder to shoulder she 'nd I wend,
Eyes to eyes, our topics extend.
Not for a big dinner we meet;
With zephyr we go in retreat.

见　春

料峭春风偶转西，
丝丝垂地绿枝低。
青青含翠经年草，
溢溢生机正好时。

A View of Spring

West freezing spring wind has a chance to blow;
Wickers upon wickers droop aground low.
Emerald green is the bygone years' grass;
Vigorous and powerful it does grow.

清平乐

韶华春半，
微雨繁花乱。
落了万瑛香未远，
唯惹伊心灿烂。

十年水北云烟。
平生华发苍颜。
会遇文人墨客，
与谈更广江山。

The Pure Serene Tune

The spring of mine half gone,
Light rain makes blooms fall on and on.
As the flowers drop, sweetness remains near;
The sweetness but fills me with cheer.

Ten years here I cannot retrace,
With my hair grey and weathered face.
I meet scholars and learned men,
From whom I know keenly more then.

清 明

蒙蒙河岸柳依依，
紫燕轻飞觅新泥。
最爱清明别样绿，
睐眸但诉草萋萋。

At the Clear and Bright

On the river bank march misty willows;
In search of new mud fly purple swallows.
I love such a green of Clear and Bright best;
My eyes half closed, I tell of lush meadows.

清　明

清明前日雨纷纷，
道阻而长拜母亲。
严考长眠双墩墓，
屈膝叩拜未见人。

The Tomb Sweeping Day

It rained and rained two days before the Day;
We went tomb-sweeping over a long way.
My father rests in the Shuangdun grave yard;
I could not see him though I kowtoued hard.

立冬（其一）

秋尽冬初至，
丹枫叶遂沉。
凌霜菊怒放，
异客倍思人。

The Beginning of Winter (No. 1)

Autumn's out with the cold winter in;
The maple leaves fall down herein.
Against frost mums furiously blow;
In the alien land I miss kin.

立冬(其二)

秋往至寒冬，
丹枫叶落红。
菊当霜傲放，
人远客思浓。

The Beginning of Winter (No. 2)

Autumn ends as winter arrives;
The maple leaves then spin or fall.
Against frost th' chrysanthemum thrives;
Far from home he misses dear all.

秋 思

方安半月便成秋，
日做羹汤总盼休。
惟愿匆匆三载去，
浅清岁月但悠悠。

My Thought in Fall

I've just lived here half a month and it's fall;
I cook all day hoping for rest at all.
I only wish such days to go by fast!
But these hard days will for a long while last.

令君词

春华徐淡她绝色，
滚滚红尘俏婉颜。
清句芳词一曲曲，
鹧鸪红袖两翩翩。

Ode to Lingjun

With the passage of time she looks her best;
In the earthly world she has looks so blessed,
Poems and lyrics done line after line,
Her *A Partridge in the Sky* more than nine.

冷清秋（其一）

青鸦茂木居，
山野漫黄菊。
红叶枫枝落，
流溪挽岫曲。

The Late Autumn Days (No. 1)

The thick wood is the grey crow's home;
Hills and plains chrysanthemums roam.
Fall the maple twigs and leaves red;
Along winding hills the stream's led.

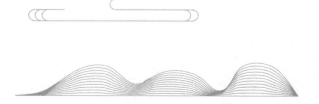

冷清秋（其二）

茂木住青鸦，
黄菊遍野花。
纷纷枫叶落，
远岫带溪发。

The Late Autumn Days (No. 2)

Grey crows live amid the deep trees;
Across th' field brown flowers one sees.
Maple leaves fall one after one;
From far hills the stream starts to run.

问扬州

暗尘看尽恼心愁，
意气不羁怎可休。
怒马飞驰十几载，
无能渡己叹风流。

A Question to Yangzhou

All the dirt I've seen with a mind of gloom;
Spirits high, how can I let them not boom?
Galloping like th' horse eighteen years to vie,
I can't ferry myself but heave a sigh.

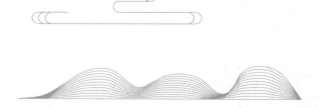

·参考书目·

[1] 王国维. 人间词话[M]. 范雅编著. 南京:江苏人民出版社,
    2016.
[2] 王力. 王力谈诗词格律[M]. 南京:江苏人民出版社,2019.
[3] 吴战垒. 中国诗学[M]. 上海:东方出版社,2021.
[4] 许渊冲译. 唐诗三百首[M]. 北京:五洲传播出版社,2012.
[5] 赵彦春译. 英韵唐诗百首[M]. 北京:高等教育出版社,2019.
[6] 朱光潜. 诗论[M]. 上海:华东师范大学出版社,2018.